garet Tempest.

Moldy Warp the Mole was first published
in Great Britain by William Collins Sons & Co 1940

This edition published by HarperCollins*Publishers* 2000
Abridged text copyright © The Alison Uttley Literary Property Trust 2000
Illustrations copyright © The Estate of Margaret Tempest 2000
Copyright this arrangement © HarperCollins*Publishers* 2000
Additional illustration by Mark Burgess
Little Grey Rabbit ® and the Little Grey Rabbit logo are
trademarks of HarperCollins*Publishers* Limited

1 3 5 7 9 10 8 6 4 2

ISBN: 000 198389-X

The HarperCollins website address is: www.**fire**and**water**.com

Printed and bound in Singapore

MOLDY WARP
THE MOLE

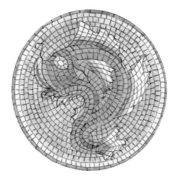

ALISON UTTLEY
Pictures by Margaret Tempest

Collins
An Imprint of HarperCollins*Publishers*

MOLDY WARP sat in his armchair one morning, examining a tiny square stone. It was painted with a golden eye which seemed to watch the Mole wherever he went. It looked at him when he cooked his mushroom breakfast, when he made his hard little bed, and when he polished his pennies.

"Where this came from there will be the rest of the picture," he thought. "There are only two creatures who could tell me about it. One is Wise Owl, who is asleep by day and fierce by night. The other is Brock the Badger, and where he lives nobody knows."

Moldy Warp washed the small stone in the stream
which conveniently ran along the floor of his
room, and he rubbed it on his sleeve.

"Now this is an eye of long ago," said Mole to himself. "It belonged to somebody's picture book – a stone picture book. I've not found any treasure since I made Owl's bell. I'll go to Hearthstone Pasture and see if I can find anything more of it."

He took his bright spade from the corner, and brushed his hair and whiskers. Then he went round his house to lock all the back doors. There were thirteen of them, each leading to a different molehill.

Mole went down the passage to the front door. This led him out near the holly tree. He cut a short stick and started up the fields with the spade and a bag on his back.

He hadn't gone far when he saw an animal leaping across the field, trying to catch his slender shadow.

"Hallo, Hare!" cried the Mole. "What's the matter?"

"I'm a Mad March Hare!" shouted Hare. "I'm always like this when the March wind blows. I can't help it."

"But it's the month of May," objected Mole.

"It may be May! But there's a March wind, forgotten by somebody, blowing in this field. Where are you going with that spade and sack, Moldy Warp?"

Mole hesitated. He didn't really want Hare's company. Then his good temper overcame him.

"I'm going treasure hunting," said he.

"Oh Moldy Warp! Can I go with you?" Hare quivered with excitement.

"Yes," sighed Mole.

"I'll run ahead and save your short legs, Moldy," said Hare, and he galloped off and was soon out of sight. Mole plodded slowly on his way.

In the next field a little figure stooped here and there, and Mole recognised little Grey Rabbit.

"Cuckoo!" he called. The rabbit ran with a glad cry to meet him.

"I was gathering cowslips to make a cowslip ball," said she. "Where are you going, Moldy Warp?"

"I'm going on a treasure hunt," replied Mole.

"Can I come with you?" she asked. Then she stopped. "It isn't like a fox hunt, is it?"

"Not at all," said Mole. "It's like hunt the thimble, deep down in the ground."

She walked by his side, talking of cowslip balls and cherry pie and fox's gloves. Every now and then she stopped to gather another cowslip. Mole went solemnly on, and, with a light scutter of feet she caught him up.

Then Squirrel came bounding from a nut tree.

"Hallo! Where are you two going?"

"Treasure hunting," said Grey Rabbit happily. "Come along Squirrel and help to carry it."

"I'm not dressed for treasure hunting," said Squirrel, and she stooped over a pool and stuck a cowslip in her dress. "I ought to have put on my new ribbon."

Then she scampered after Grey Rabbit, and
walked by her side, eagerly whispering to her.

Shrill laughter and cries came from over a wall, and there, playing in the cornfield was a crowd of small rabbits.

They came scampering up to the Mole as he crawled through a hole in the wall. "Please, Sir, what time is it?" they asked.

Before Mole could look at the sun, Grey Rabbit replied, "Half-past kissing time, and time to kiss again."

All the little rabbits rubbed their noses, and trotted after little Grey Rabbit.

"Where is Mole going?" they whispered.

"Sh-sh-sh," Grey Rabbit lowered her voice. "He's going treasure hunting."

Mole led them through a shady lane along little paths that only animals know.

Then the procession passed through a field.

Out of the thick grass came Hedgehog with two pails of milk.

"Hallo! Moldy Warp, and little Grey Rabbit and Squirrel, and all you little 'uns! Where are you going so fast this morning?" he asked.

"Treasure hunting," replied Mole.

"I'll go along with you," said Hedgehog. "Come here, Fuzzypeg," he called. The shy little fellow came out of the grass with a butterfly net. "Come treasure hunting. You can help to catch it if it flies away."

Soon they were joined by the Speckledy Hen and some fieldmice, all eager to hunt.

"There's rather a crowd," sighed Moldy Warp. "I shall be glad to get underground."

At last they got to Hearthstone Pasture, where dark rocks lay on the smooth grass like black sheep.

"This is where I found my little square stone," Mole told them. "It was underneath the old hawthorn tree. Now wait while I go down and hunt for the treasure."

The animals sat round the tree and watched him. He took his sharp spade and began to dig. Then he seized his sack and wriggled down into the earth out of sight.

"Let's have a treasure hunt, too," cried Squirrel. "And Grey Rabbit shall give a prize."

So they all ran about the field peering among the rocks, poking their noses into crannies, sniffing and seeking.

One rabbit found a jay's feather, and another a wren's nest. Some found flowers and ladybirds, and one found a silk bag full of spider's eggs.

"Look what I've found," called Squirrel, and she pointed to Hare, fast asleep under a rock.

"Where's the treasure?" he cried, rubbing his eyes.

"The prize is won by Fuzzypeg," announced little Grey Rabbit, and she showed his find. It was a four-leafed clover.

"What is the prize?" asked Hare.

"The cowslip ball," said Grey Rabbit, who had been industriously threading the cowslips on a grass. She gave the yellow flowery ball to Fuzzypeg, who tossed it up in the air and caught it.

"The young rabbits ought to go home," said Grey Rabbit, "and Fuzzypeg. It's getting late."

"Oh no! Let us stay up tonight," they implored.

"We can't desert old Mole," said Fuzzypeg.

"Let us call him," suggested little Grey Rabbit.

So they all put their paws to their mouths and gave the hide-and-seek cry, "Cuckoo. Cherry tree. Moldy Warp, you can't see me."

A blue veil of darkness slowly covered the fields.

The rabbits clustered round Grey Rabbit, and the youngest one clung to her skirt.

"I'm cold," he whimpered.

"Let us make a tent and all get inside," said Grey Rabbit.

Squirrel gathered long pointed leaves from a
chestnut tree, and Hare stood on tiptoe to pull
branches of flowery May.

The little fieldmice took their needles and cottons from their pockets, and sewed the leaves with tiny stitches, white and small as their own teeth.

Grey Rabbit pinned the strips together with thorn pins, and Hedgehog fixed a tent pole in the ground. Soon there was a fine leafy tent, sprinkled with hawthorn blossoms and prickly with thorns, standing in the field.

They all crept into the tent and cuddled together. Little Grey Rabbit told them the story of a white rabbit named Cinderella, who went to a ball, and lost her glass slipper.

The little animals closed their eyes and fell asleep.

"Snuff! Sniff! I smell Rabbit," muttered a Fox.

He glided round the little tent. "Here's a little green bush where no tree used to be." He put his nose close to the leaves and opened his mouth.

"I'll puff and I'll huff and I'll blow their little house down," he muttered. But the prickles of Old Hedgehog stuck in his chin, and the spikes of little Fuzzypeg scratched his nose, and all the thorns of the tent ran into his skin.

"It's a trap," grumbled the Fox, and he ran off.

Now all this time Mole was underground. He went along smooth winding paths, up steps and down, through a little door and into a room. On the floor stood a stone crock filled with gold.

"Am I dreaming?" he asked himself.

Footsteps padded near, and a large Badger entered the room. "Moldy Warp! How did you get here? I've never had a visitor in all my life!" exclaimed the Badger.

He lighted a lantern and Mole blinked his dim eyes with amazement. On the floor was a picture of a blue and green dolphin. It was made of bright little square stones, but one tiny stone was missing. The lovely dolphin had only one eye.

Mole brought out his little stone. It exactly fitted, like a square in a puzzle.

"The missing eye, lost for many years!" cried Badger excitedly. "Thank you! Only a wise Mole could have found the ancient Dolphin's eye."

31

Then Badger held up his lantern to a cupboard in the wall and showed Moldy Warp his treasures. On the shelves were tiny figures, all carved out of coloured stones, gold necklaces and glass beads.

"How beautiful they are!" cried Mole.

"You shall have a few to take to your own house, Moldy Warp," replied Badger.

Mole modestly chose a little grey stone rabbit, but the Badger lifted down little animals of jade and amber and dropped them into Mole's sack.

"They will do for doorstops for your fourteen doors, Moldy Warp," said he. "And here's the crock of gold."

Mole thanked him, and shook his great paw.

"Come and have some supper," said the Badger.

He drew a jug of heather ale, and cut a hunch of sweet herb bread and some slices of cold ham. Then by the light of the lantern, the two ate and drank.

"Your health, Badger," said Mole, sipping the heather ale. "My! This is good!"

"Made from a long-forgotten recipe," said the Badger. "I'll give you a pitcher of it to carry home."

Then the Badger talked of days of long ago, when the Romans came to England and made the stone picture floors, such as Mole had seen.

As he talked, Mole's eyes began to close, his head nodded, and he dropped off to sleep.

When he awoke he lay in a truckle bed, tucked up with linen sheets. He looked around for Badger, but the great animal had gone. Mole picked up his bag and crock, put the spade on his shoulder, and clasped the jug of heather ale.

He wandered along the confusing maze of passages, until at last he found himself in the open field.

He trotted as fast as he could to the hawthorn tree, calling, "Coo-oo. Coo-oo!"

Hedgehog put his head through the tent opening and saw Mole.

"Here he is! Here's lost Moldy Warp!" he shouted, and the rest came tumbling after him into the field.

"Have you found the treasure, Moldy Warp?" they cried excitedly. Mole opened his sack and emptied out the little cocks, the jade hedgehogs, the amber rabbits and a squirrel of green bronze.

"Oh my!" cried the little rabbits and fieldmice.

"Where did you find these?" asked Grey Rabbit.

Mole shook his head. "It's a secret that can never be told," he said.

Then all the animals insisted on helping to carry Mole's treasure. Each one took a precious little toy, and galloped off down the fields.

"Be careful!" he called. But they ran faster than ever, eager to get home.

Some dropped their treasure in the long grass, and some lost them in the hedgerows. The fieldmice threw theirs away because they were too heavy. Hedgehog left his jade hedgehog in the cowshed, and the cow ate it with her hay.

Hare leapt over a gorse
bush and the amber hare
fell from his pocket.
Squirrel put her bronze
squirrel on a wall and
forgot about it.

Little Grey Rabbit carried the pitcher of
heather ale without spilling a drop. She left it at
Mole's front door, and hurried home to cook
breakfast for Squirrel and Hare.

"Ah me!" sighed the Mole, when he arrived hours later. "I'm glad I carried my crock of gold myself."

He waddled slowly into his pantry with the heather ale.

"That's safe, thanks to Grey Rabbit," said he.

He polished the gold coins on his fur sleeve till they shone and looked admiringly at the pictures of eagles and lions engraved upon them.

There was a rat-tat-tat at the door and he went to open it.

"They are all very sorry they lost your treasures,
Moldy Warp," said little Grey Rabbit, stepping
in with Old Hedgehog's milk pail full of flowers.
"They have sent you these instead."

She filled a jug with silver daisies and golden buttercups.

"You like them just as much, don't you, Moldy Warp?" she asked wistfully.

"More, much more," answered the Mole. "What is a precious stone to a living flower?" Yet he gave a deep sigh.

He put his hand in his pocket and brought out his forgotten little stone rabbit. He put it in the middle of the mantelpiece and Grey Rabbit stood on tiptoes to look at it.

"I'm going to give a picnic to all the animals who kindly waited for me in that cold wild pasture up there on the hill," said Mole. "Please ask them to come tomorrow afternoon, Grey Rabbit."

Little Grey Rabbit ran to spread the good news.

The next day they all appeared, dressed in their best clothes. There was Mole ready for them, with the tablecloth spread out on the daisies and the jug of flowers in the middle.

He had provided wild raspberries, rosepetal jam, bluebell jelly, lettuces and tiny red carrots.

"Your very good health, Moldy Warp," called Hare, as he sipped the sun-filled honey ale which filled the tiny glasses.

"Good health! Good luck!" cried the others.

Mole nodded and smiled and sat back with his velvet coat glossy in the sunshine. What a lot of good friends he had, to be sure!